Is The Real French Kiss

A Guide To Having Erotic Butt Play

Tori Silks

Table of Contents

Erotic Story…My Lover Gives Me A Morning Ass Licking

Chapter 1…What Is Analingus?

Chapter 2…It's Really Just Another Way To Play

Chapter 3…Why Does Analingus Feels Erotic

Chapter 4…Calming The Big Fear: Coming In Contact With Fecal Material

Chapter 5…So, Let's Have Some Fun Without Fear

Chapter 6…Analingus Techniques and Tips

Chapter 7…Simple Analingus Positions

Chapter 8…Analingus is Anal Foreplay

Chapter 9…Performing The Art of Analingus On Your Wife

Chapter 10…Moving From Analingus To Anal Fingering   What About Analingus

Chapter 11…Let's Finish The Book With Another Erotic Scene…Eating Her Sweet Ass

Read this erotic story and if you would like this to be a reality in your life like it is in mine. This book will teach you how to make it a reality.

Erotic Story

My Lover Gives Me A Morning Ass Licking

I woke up on my stomach hearing the alarm clock at 7:15am. I looked over at my husband and lifted up a little to scoot over closer to him who was lying on his back. It was a beautiful Saturday morning, and we have nothing planned to do all day. I passionately kissed him after saying good morning lover then smiled at him, knowing what that type of kiss meant. It was to let him know I wanted him to do what I find irresistible for him to do for me in the morning. I'm such a lucky lady that he loves to do it as well.

I fell back onto my stomach while spreading my legs wider, while at the same time I pulled a pillow up under my stomach as I bent my knees up a little lifting my ass up in the air for his taking. I was preparing a backdoor buffet for him to feast on this morning. I had taken the time to use a wet wipe to wipe my ass really good before I even scooted closer to him. He got the message and then he crawled up behind me grabbing hold of my legs still wrapped in the black fishnet stockings from the erotic sex session we just had the night before.

I had my ass lifted up in the air, and I buried my head into my pillow as I felt his warm dripping tongue briskly move over and lick my tender asshole. I groaned and sighed as I took extreme pleasure in his tongue beginning to move all over my ass crease. I could also feel his saliva starting to coat my asshole. He was moaning persistently as he gave me the impression that he tremendously loved licking on my asshole for me as much as I loved him doing it. But I know I'm a fortunate wife that has a husband that loves oral sex of any kind. He once licked my ass from the side as he tenderly fingered my pussy for over an hour.

This morning I said to him, "That's it, baby tell me you love licking my ass."

He replied with his face still buried in my ass cheeks, "Ummmm, baby I love licking your ass, your ass is so.... delicious and, um umm it's so wonderful and tastes so good."

I then added, "Ya baby, let me hear you worship my tight little asshole while you lick me honey."

He then began to go on and on about how much he loved it while he consumed my wrinkled starfish passionately. I had never considered having anyone actually lick my asshole before I married this amazing man. He is such an erotic lover and had just started doing it to me. I remember the shock and awe I had when I first felt what he was doing to my asshole with his tongue. He also said he had never done it to anybody else before, but he wanted to do it for me. He said for some reason or other he couldn't resist the desire to always stick his tongue there while he's eating my cunt out. And I have to tell you those first years we were together he was eating my cunt for me almost every day if you can believe that.

I'm not really into getting fucked in the ass although we have done it a few times. But the shear depravity of having him loving to lick on my asshole really turns me on to the ultimate levels. I'd never thought I'd have such a loving man like him being so willing and eager to want to lick on my butt hole. He doesn't care about the smell or taste he says he loves doing it anyways. Although I must say that I do keep it quite clean for him just in case he has the urge for the backdoor buffet that day.

I started setting my alarm clock for 45 minutes early so that I can have enough time in the morning to let him fully clean out my asshole for me with that lovely tongue of his. He loves licking my asshole almost more than I adore him licking it, so I never have to hesitate to ask him to lick it for me.

I cherish going to bed with my man and waking up to his tongue in my asshole. I have him lick me slowly and softly for about 15-20 minutes until I'm completely awake and then he can begin licking both my holes as eagerly as he wants until I cum all over his face. Yes, I'm a squirter in case you were wondering.

Today was no different as for about 20 minutes I lied there with my ass in the air and my mouth open moaning softly, as I lightly held the back of his head with one hand and the pillow with the other.

After 20 minutes of his tender soft tongue licking and munching on my asshole it was over. I was grabbing the pillow and his head tightly yelling for him to lick me faster and harder, and to dig his tongue deep into both of my holes until I finally orgasmed all over his face close to 8 o'clock. After I did, I looked back at him still indulging in my tender holes and I felt so delighted at his love for my asshole and pussy that I pulled his head out my ass and rolled over onto my back and said,

9

"Oh, yesssss, I love that baby so much, as he finished drinking up my juices. Then he said let's get up and go to the beach and get some breakfast."

If you enjoyed this true story, you could have some erotic sexual adventures as well. In this book I'm going to teach you some proper ways to eat your mate's ass to give them the ultimate pleasure. In my opinion that is what married sex is all about, giving your mate the ultimate pleasure. I'll also give you some safe ways to do it if you are saying yuck! But believe me this can be one of the most erotic experiences you can share in the bedroom with the one you love. You will also find out why I call it the "The Real French Kiss."

Chapter 1

What Is Analingus?

The term analingus is also known as rimming, or giving a rim job, or in some circles it's called tossing the salad. To put it bluntly, It is quite simply the physical act of licking or inserting your tongue into the anus to provide sexual pleasure for your lover. Some even call it the black or brown kiss. I call it the "Real" French Kiss. It is true that not everybody feels comfortable with even the thought of kissing or licking their lover's anus. Or with having it done to them as well. But the fact is, many lovers are extremely curious about oral-anal contact.

Analingus also casually called "rimming" was not even on my list of sexual activities when I was younger. And I must say that I was really surprised at first, but when I actually tried it, I thought it was truly amazing. You too sister, like me could become enthusiastic about it as well if you will only put down the stigmas and give it a try one day. Simply, just let your man do it once to you and you will be addicted to the amazing feeling of having your ass licked by the love of your life.

Many lovers like my husband had an accidental introduction to analingus during an amazing cunnilingus session. Since the bottom of the vaginal entrance is really close to the anus he just went ahead and licked it for me one day as well. He heard me moan as his tongue barely touched my asshole. That one time when he was giving me cunnilingus was all it took. And he always wants to please me, so he continued to lick and poke with his tongue in my ass and soon this became a very regular occurrence in our oral love making play.

Sometimes just a little lick that is actually meant for the lower vagina slips further south than it was actually intended. And the recipient immediately experiences unexpected delight like me. And sometimes this creates a surprisingly powerful urge to explore analingus a little further. We went from never do it to now almost always we do some kind of anal play when with we make love.

For other lovers, the interest in rimming develops from intentionally doing anal play. The most popular anal activities that couples try are doing a sphincter massage or fingering the anus tenderly with a lubed finger. Also, so many people are like me who also enjoy butt plugs and penis-anus intercourse.

Once we went on vacation and I decided to wear a lubed butt plug for a long three-hundred-mile interstate highway drive. We stopped periodically each hundred miles so I could insert a larger size plug in the restroom all along the way. All this effort so I would be ready for my husband once we finally get to the motel room for the night. I was so horny I wanted to be ready to have some actual anal action with his cock. Every bump in the road sent me into erotic heaven from the vibration that the plug was giving me in my ass. Trust me, it was an amazing ride, I can't tell you how many times I cummed without ever touching my clit. When we got there, I was so hot from all the stimulation that I was really ready for his tongue and cock. Try it sometime sister I promise you that you will love it!

Chapter 2

It's Really Just Another Way
To Play

Every married couple wants to keep their sex life alive, spicy, and thriving full of kinkiness. Married couples sex lives sometimes need some extra spice after years of doing it with the same person.

Anal play is simply like doing something else in the marriage bed. There is absolutely nothing wrong with or abnormal about rimming someone's asshole. If you feel tempted to condemn it, remember that, not too long ago, oral sex was considered a disgusting perversion only done by prostitutes and was outlawed in many states. Now oral sex is so widely accepted that about three-quarters of all adults say they have performed it on their lover and also had it performed on them. In fact, many couples like my husband and I don't make love without it.

Of course, rimming the anus may not ever actually become as popular as oral sex. But in the most recent years people have started to become somewhat way more sexually active with their lovers and also more experimental in their bedrooms. In fact, many surveys that have been taken suggest that around fifteen percent of all adults and that's more than twenty million people have experienced some form of anal sex play in their bedrooms.

There are actually no true statistics specifically on anal rimming, but as I personally believe as people become more comfortable with sexual experimentation in general, and anal play in particular, it should come as no big surprise that many heterosexual marriages are expressing their curiosity about analingus. Let's look at what the attraction is in the next chapter.

Chapter 3

Why Does Analingus Feel So Erotic

Many people often ask what's the big deal with anal play? Why would someone want to do such a thing to someone's asshole? Well before you get all high and mighty and too condescending about doing it you must hear some amazing facts. These are true stats that many scientists have also found out. Did you know that there are more bacteria in the human mouth than there is in the human asshole?

So, with this new important information that you have just received are you suddenly going to give up kissing your lover as well. The truth is and trust me on this one, it is so great to have your asshole touched because the anus and the surrounding tissue around it are richly endowed with nerves that are highly sensitive to gentle, playful, loving touches. The same is true for the lips and the tongue. So, when you put these areas together, the combination can be powerfully erotic for a couple, no matter who is doing the licking.

Another major reason anal stimulation feels so great and erotic is because of the pelvic floor muscles. These are the muscles that lie beneath the surface of the anal area. These muscles also play an important role in having great sex and are the ones that contract during an orgasm. So, whether you are using a sex toy, finger or even your tongue to massage or insert into the anus, it stimulates those pelvic floor muscles and heightens the overall erotic sensations.

Finally, the very act of having sex alone between a couple draws a good deal of its emotional power from both lovers' having a wholehearted acceptance of each other. Analingus involves acceptance of an area that's often not accepted with a couple. In fact, it's one place on the human body that's usually rejected by most couples. Analingus simply becomes a way for the giver to say to their mate "I love all of you. No part of your wonderful body turns me off." And it's a way for the receiver to say:" I'm totally yours. No part of me is off limits to you." And believe me this level of mutual acceptance can be a powerful turn-on for a couple that is in love.

So, if you're interested in rimming your lover's ass, please, talk it over with them before you just dive in and start licking. Some couples may even prefer to discuss sexual experimentation with their mate in a nonsexual setting. Others like my husband and me like to discuss experimentation while we're actually making love. This has worked great for us over the years.

Once I was on my knees taking his cock in my mouth and trying to swallow his whole cock. He reached to the back of my head and entwined his fingers in my hair on the back on my head and pushed his cock into my throat. Instantly I came as he penetrated my throat.

I learn that day that I wanted him to fuck my face by suing my face as a pussy and pushing my head past the comfort zone when I am sucking him off. It really turns me on when he does this, somedays I can't hardly wait to get on my knees. So please don't be afraid to raise the issue in whatever way feels the most comfortable to you in your relationship.

If you and your lover have open and frank sexual communication, and I'm sorry if this offends you, but if you are married you should. You might simply announce to them one day during dinner or while you are watching TV that you'd like to try analingus sometime. On the other hand, if you feel reluctant to admit your interest in this type of sexual play, and that's the case for many people believe me, you might raise the issue indirectly. Perhaps by simply mentioning offhandedly that you had read something about it on a website this morning and ask what your lover thinks of it.

You know your spouse better than anyone else so if your honey grimaces at the thought of it, chances are that analingus won't ever become a part of your intimate repertoire. Be sure to definitely never pressure a lover to try rimming if he or she doesn't want to do it. But if your lover shows any interest at all, even if it's covered in skepticism and concern about hygiene, you may detect enough of an opening to pursue the issue further with them at another time. Just simply allay your lover's concerns and perhaps introduce it into your lovemaking practices.

If you as a couple in love decide to experiment with analingus, you also need to discuss who's interested in which role. Some people are interested in only one side of any rimming interaction. While others feel equally comfortable in both roles. Before you begin, be sure you clear the air on who does what.

Chapter 4

Calming The Big Fear: Coming In Contact With Fecal Material

Because looking at how the anus is designed, we can know for sure that God originally designed the anus for outward action. And also, because the anus is intimately involved in defecation, many people assume that oral-anal contact must involve contact with human feces. Of course, this is always a real possibility when you do it. Even with good wiping practices, some traces of fecal material may cling to the anus and the skin around it.

However, many scientists still insists that the anus, or anal canal and rectum usually contain surprisingly very little amounts of stool. Most fecal material is stored above the rectum in the descending colon. When stool finally does moves down into the rectum, you feel "the urge to go to the bathroom," and it then passes out of the body fairly quickly. That's why most of the time, when you feel no urge to defecate, there are only slight trace amounts of stool in the rectum, anal canal, and anus. And these traces can easily be washed out with a warm cloth.

But if you are really concerned simply use a soft bathroom wipe to clean your anus right before you let them, go down on you. I personally have done this countless times. Some people also have concerns about what is called the Infection connection. And to be real this is actually a good concern. It's really important to consider there is the possibility of analingus exposing the giver to digestive tract bacteria. The digestive tract is the home to millions of bacteria that assist in digestion, notably known as E. coli. These micro-organisms get incorporated into our stool and can be found in and around the anus. Although they do help with digestion, they might also cause infection. If E. coli comes in contact with the vagina or urethra, the woman might develop a terrible vaginal yeast infection or maybe a urinary tract infection also known as a UTI, which is a cystitis or bladder infection. That's why a standard recommendation is that anything that comes into contact with the person's anus should not touch the vulva or vagina afterwards.

The human digestive tract might also contain other harmful micro-organisms that can be spread during oral-anal contact. Among them are of course other bacteria. Two significant germs are Shigella and Salmonella, which is was causes food poisoning. These germs can cause acute and often vicious diarrhea. And it's possible for someone with mild symptoms to transmit the infection to someone else who develops more severe symptoms.

Also, intestinal parasites, notably Giardia lamblia, and amoebas, both of which cause diarrhea.

Other various viruses, notably HIV *(which is more commonly known as the AIDS virus)* and the one that causes hepatitis A. HIV typically spreads through blood-to-blood contact. Anal tissue can bleed easily if it is ruptured. It is estimated that one-third of American adults have hemorrhoids. These varicose veins of the anal canal sometimes cause extreme pain, but frequently do not, so affected individuals may not even know they have them. If HIV-contaminated blood enters the mouth of someone who has a minor injury such as bleeding gums, the infection might be transmitted to them. All of these things seem so bad but it is possible to have fun with this great erotic play without fear and the next chapter will tell how.

Chapter 5

So, Let's Have Some Fun Without Fear

Because so many infections can be transmitted to you during analingus, it's important to only participate in anal activity with someone you know really well like a spouse. It's crucial my friend that lovers who want to play this way take prudent precautions:

First simply make sure you wash your anal areas thoroughly. Before any sexual encounter involving oral-anal play. Make sure the whole area around and even inside the anus should be carefully washed with antibacterial soap and water and a warm cloth.

For even some more erotic fun and a good prelude to this pleasure you might want to consider the both of you showering together. Each of you tenderly taking the time and washing each other's private areas really good while showering together is even better. Not only is it sensual foreplay, but you can both actually make sure everything is clean and ready to go down there.

Clean It Up Down There Really Good

It may be just me but I personally believe if you're going to ask someone to stick their tongue in your butt, you should at least show them the courtesy of making it nice and clean for them. Often, a bath is all you need, and a shared bath before anal fun makes for some great foreplay as well, while helping both partners to simply relax with each other.

Maybe you might want to even consider giving yourself an enema. For an extra margin of hygiene safety, the recipient might want to try an enema before washing. Enemas rinse the whole rectum and anal canal, removing most traces of any fecal material. They are also very easy to use by yourself, especially the cheap disposable enemas available over the counter from pharmacies or even Walmart. Simply put some lube on the tip and insert the flexible nozzle into your anus while you are on your hands and knees and gently squeeze the bottle. This pushes the fluid into the rectum at a good angle. After a few minutes, simply sit on the toilet and allow the fluid to drain out. The bottle can then be refilled with warm water and reused if you would like to repeat the process again. My husband and I almost always use an enema before any serious anal play just to make sure things are completely empty down there and we don't have any surprise visits from a lonely turd.

But if you'd prefer to just dive in, in the heat of the moment, you should at least keep some clean wipes handy beside the bed. Use the type of wipes that are absorbent and alcohol-free, and they kill most bacteria, fungi and viruses. They're really ideal for quick and easy bedside hygiene.

Although it's not really necessary, some people like us prefer to do a deeper cleaning. In this case, you may want to try an anal douche or an enema. Enemas can also be enjoyable in themselves, whether the goal is hygiene, or sensation. A good anal douche has a ribbed nozzle designed to make cleaning your butt more fun. For a one-time use, you can also use a Saline enema that is sold in the drugstores. Once again, enemas and douches can be fun on their own terms, but they're not at all necessary to enjoying safe analingus.

Maybe Use Dental Dams

Just Dam It Up!

As we have said the asshole can harbor some very serious bacteria. If you want to have anal play as safely as possible, you can always just dam it up!   A dental dam is a simple latex barrier that is used during anal sex. It also will allow you to enjoy kissing and tonguing your lover's butt, while lowering your chances of encountering some really nasty bugs.

So, you might want to consider using a dam to dam it up. Dental dams are often thin sheets of latex rubber that work like a condom does. When in place they act as a physical barrier between the anus and the mouth. They may feel awkward to use at first, but, like condoms, they can be incorporated into analingus easily with a little practice and maybe even a sense of humor. Dental dams are available at most pharmacies, or you can simply buy some unlubricated condoms or even latex gloves and cut them into flat sheets to use. Another alternative that is quite effective is a sheet of cling film *(Saran Wrap has so many bedrooms uses! Make sure to use the non-microwaveable variety.)* Simply spread a thin sheet along your partner's butt cheeks and crack, then put a little dollop of lube on the inside, and dive in. To heighten pleasure even more for them, massage a little of the sexual lubricant into your lover's anus before applying the dam to it.

Be sure to completely rinse the anus afterwards. After doing analingus without a dam, be sure to rinse your mouth with an antiseptic mouthwash or, at the very least, some water. In truly monogamous couples, where both people are confident that neither has hepatitis, HIV or intestinal parasites, the only real risk of analingus is contact with some type of digestive bacteria. Simple enemas and careful washing of the whole area virtually eliminates any worry of this as well. According to many doctors, healthy, monogamous couples who practice careful anal hygiene, the risk of doing analingus causing infection or illness is "extremely low." Consider your own situation carefully. Discuss it over thoroughly with your lover and then you two decide for yourselves what the appropriate level of precautions you want to take.

Okay Just Kiss My Ass!

Let's face it folks, butts are really sexy. And pretty little wrinkled buttholes are just as sexy as well. Just like penises, and pussies assholes come in all kinds of colors, shapes, and sizes. Anal sex is on the rise in popularity, but few people will dare explore or discuss the fine art of practicing analingus. And that's a real shame for most, because a well-executed rim job is a thing of joy for couples to dive in together. But if licking the butthole is not for you then you can spend your erotic times together but just kissing the butt cheeks all over and giving them pleasure by also licking them with your tongue.

Go Ahead And Tease It!

If you or your lover are new to analingus, you may want to build up to the most intimate French Kiss. Try teasing them with your finger first, or slowly kissing and licking your way along their butt cheeks. As with any kind of sex, it's better to warm up before any penetration. If your partner is new to the sensation, try turning up the heat by using your hands on their genitals. If the wife is doing it to her husband, then simply play with his cock, while getting him used to the feeling of your tongue near his butthole. For the husband doing it to his wife, tenderly massage her clit, or pleasure her G-Spot with your fingers.

It's Okay To Kiss It!

When your lover is finally relaxed and totally aroused, use your lips like you would on any other part of their body. Lick along the crack of their ass, as you plant small kisses along their cheeks. My husband loves to lick the string of my thong going up my ass crack between my cheeks. Blow lightly on their butthole. Then tenderly stick your tongue where the sun doesn't shine. Be sure to also come up for air and check in with your lover periodically. If you plan to make rimming a regular part of your sexual diet, you wanna make sure you get the recipe just right.

Chapter 6

Analingus Techniques and Tips

One thing to always try to remember about any type of anal play is that when you are first getting started take it really slow. I mean painfully slow. Some recipients enjoy having their lover plunge right into analingus. But unless they specifically request it, you should always approach this highly sensitive area of their privates very slowly. Just softly massage, kiss, and lick their lower back, thighs, hips, and buttocks as you slowly work your way inward towards his or her anus. A slow approach builds their anticipation for what's about to happen and often heightens the eroticism of analingus.

Then carefully use your lips, and gently kiss your lover's anus with a regular kiss. Be sure to kiss the whole area around the asshole as well for it is all erotic. After you have thoroughly kissed their anal area and I mean thoroughly then be sure to use the flat of your tongue to press it against the outside of your partner's anus.

Then after you have massaged the outside with the flat of your tongue thoroughly just press the very tip of your tongue into it. Wiggle it around a little in the anus, and softly slip it inside and move it in and out or wiggle it around in circles. This is quite erotic sexual action my friend. And your spouse knows that you truly love them to French Kiss them this way.

Whatever you and your lover ultimately decide about analingus, discussing it openly can deepen the intimacy you both share together. You will learn more about yourself and each other. You will become clearer about what you're willing and unwilling to try in the marriage bed. And in the end, as it were, these intimate discussions will help you feel closer to one another and better able to experience whatever sexual pleasure you both want to enjoy in your marriage. I actually believe the act of analingus can actually bring a couple closer together. After all you are sharing your most intimate part of your body with them.

Chapter 7

Simple Analingus Positions

Just like any sexual act of love making there are certain positions that allow for some great oral-anal contact with a minimum of contortions. The positions that work best for anal sex also work equally as good with analingus. These erotic positions do not require too much dexterity and also allow the giver complete access to their lover's anus. As I've mentioned, this type of sexual activity can make people a little nervous and unless your partner is relaxed, they may not even enjoy the pleasure you are trying to give them. So, be sure to take your time and be very patient with them.

The Receiver Gets On Their Knees and Elbows... The person receiving the anal pleasure simply assumes the position typically used by most for rear-entry. That is (doggie style) intercourse, while his or her lover kneels or squats behind them. Either partner may gently spread their butt cheeks to expose the anus to their lover's tongue.

The Standing Bent Over Position… The person on the receiving end stands and bends over at the waist, as his or her lover kneels, sits, or squats behind them. This is a great position for the living room or the kitchen. As the licker can sit on the couch or chair as their lover bends over in front of them. The receiver might want to lean forward against the wall or couch or even the end of the bed for that matter.

Lying Supine… The person being licked lies on his or her back, with their legs slightly bent, and their knees pulled up to their chest or spread apart in a leg sling. The licking lover squats or lies on his or her stomach between their legs. It often helps in this position to place a pillow of a wedge under the recipient's hips, which then raises the anus up and allows for easier access to their sweet little puckered hole.

The Popular Sixty-Nine........ Compared with simply mutual oral-genital contact, practicing mutual analingus requires somewhat more physical flexibility from the couple. Height differences can also make this position a little challenging as well. But many couples often enjoy this position all the more. As with my husband and I, this position may be a little challenging with our different heights of the couple. But with a little practice it can still be enjoyed.

Go Ahead And Sit On Their Face........... This is my husband's all-time favorite position to do cunnilingus on me in. This position requires the giver to simply lie on their back and the receiver to 'sit' on their partner's face. You do want to be careful that you are not suffocating your lover in this position, so it helps to simply lean forward slightly.

On Their Sides... In this position each partner can lie on their sides, and the man can lick the anus. This is kind of like the lazy doggie style, except with the anus.

The truth is you can find any position that suits you. Almost any standard intercourse position can work for anal sex, and many will work for analingus as well. Simply of you can reach the butthole you can lick it. Find the ones that work best and please both you and your partner the most! Now that we've talked about some positions, let's talk about analingus as great foreplay.

Chapter 8

Analingus is Anal Foreplay

Once you're both in position for analingus, here are some tips on great techniques for foreplay. As we've said analingus is oral-anal sex. Which as we know involves your spouse's mouth on your anus carefully using their tongue and lips to stimulate the sensitive area.

As I've mentioned before, not many people are all for you just plunging your erect penis into their rear end. It's not exactly a pleasant first-time experience for some ladies. This is where analingus becomes so important. It is an erotic way to get your partner in the mood and ready for anal sex. Simply use some light licks and kisses, then work your way up to a finger or two. After you're absolutely sure your partner can handle more, carefully move on to bigger objects such as butt plugs or small dildo's. Once your partner is fully accustomed to these foreign objects in their rear end, you can then move on to anal sex if you like. Taking this time to make sure your partner is comfortable will ensure that you get to do this again.

Practicing The Art of Analingus on Your Wife

Analingus, as we've already said, is the amazing stimulation of the anal area with the mouth and tongue by actually licking, flicking, nibbling, sucking, circling, and yes doing some tongue-probing. Many people myself included love the simple pleasure of having their anus licked or licking their lover's anus. Because the anal area is so full of nerve endings, even the tiniest sensations can register high on the turn-on meter. I love it when my husband has been licking my pussy for a long time, and getting me really turned on, then he slowly travels down and starts licking around my butthole. Oh, how I love the feeling of his tongue lightly flicking against my skin. As it just sends me over the edge!

A good way to introduce rimming is to begin by nibbling and licking your partner's buttocks. As is true for other sexual activities, it's important to explore and pleasure the whole area, rather than just diving right into the crown jewel. Once you're ready to put your mouth on the anus, and French Kiss it, start out slowly. I use my tongue to explore every little nook of my man's butthole.

Because the hole is slightly puckered, and there are a million little folds and crevices to find and lick. Aesthetically speaking, analingus need not be any more dirty or messy than cunnilingus. Just let your mouth, lips, and tongue tenderly explore your lover's anus freely, and experiment with different techniques as you go along. Listen to your lover's verbal and nonverbal responses and let those help to guide you. Some people like to really thrust their tongues in and out of their partner's anus. You can penetrate your lover's anus to absolute ecstasy.

I like to put one hand on each of his butt cheeks and spread them apart. Then, I cover his asshole with my tongue and lips, slipping the tip of my tongue just inside his ass. Rimming can be incredibly pleasurable for everyone involved, including the person giving the pleasure. So, if you're on the fence rimming is extremely, extremely pleasurable...

It's so important to keep in mind that if you're performing analingus, try to also give your mouth a good time. Again, it's never something that you're just doing to the other person; it's something you're sharing with each other.

Chapter 9

Performing The Art of Analingus on Your Wife

Okay we've said that the art of analingus is a taboo art, not conventional sexual activity by any means. Yet it is the second most powerful erogenous zone of the female body. At this point, most women who happen to be reading this, would wad this up and throw it in the fire. To them, the anus is not an erogenous zone at all ... simply because we have been trained to think this way. But to the woman who has experienced this awesome sexual pleasure for themselves, they know how sensitive this area can be if we just let our taboo feelings, and our inhibitions fall by the wayside.

There is no doubt many women on the receiving end of this wonderful tongue caress like it ...and like me they like it a lot. But to be the one providing such an act to their husband ... I wasn't so excited about that at first! I'm sure that analingus is something no decent woman would ever dream about. If that, is you, just get over yourself! I have had the dreams too.

Many women are also careful not to allow their husband to cum in their mouth while they are giving him a blow job. But those same women think nothing about coating their husband's face in their own love juice as they are cumming in his face. Even sometimes squirting in his face. If you would like to give your husband a present, check out my book *"Cunniligus Made Easy." Or my other book for you entitled "How To Make Love To His Cock With Your Mouth." Both books can up your ante in the bedroom with new skills.*

Yet ... by being on the receiving end of this intimate caress, we all learn exactly that this secret area is very sensitive. The anus, or the wife's female butthole to the experienced lover is what we could call a work of art. In my opinion there is nothing more intimate than a husband administering this erotic act to his wife. And to have the honour of receiving this intimate contact by a man who really enjoys providing it for me ... this is a form of love like on other. That's why I call it the "Real French Kiss!" Please take this next piece of advice to heart. To begin any such form of oral lovemaking, both partners need to be totally completely relaxed. Kissing the entire buttocks, including the inner thighs, should take place first. The husband administering this oral contact on his wife should spend at least 10 minutes working her over really good ... just using his lips ... and not once separating those sweet buttocks, nor using the tongue.

To do this erotic act properly, the woman receiving this contact should be lying on her tummy. While the husband is providing this contact he should be lying between his woman's legs. With his face down. His lips should completely cover every square inch of that soft creaminess of her ass cheeks. After that act has been completed, the husband might start using his tongue lightly to cover the area his lips had just burnished.

Again, this should take at least a ten-minute period, that should go something like this.

Then when she is good and hot the husband providing this sexy caress might tenderly separate her buttocks and gaze down at her sweet little tight piece of flesh, that wrinkled opening. At this point, the husband providing this erotic oral contact ... probably will be fully aroused. But he should not directly make contact with his woman's butthole just yet. Tease her a little first ... more importantly though, tease yourself as well.

Using your tongue, lick the inside of her buttocks, getting closer and closer to the areola of her butthole, but without actually touching this sweet area ...not just yet.

Learn to tease yourself as well as her. The longer you do this my friend, the more she will really enjoy this oral butt love. You might want to slide a pillow under her hips, so you have better access. But ... don't touch her butthole with your tongue just yet, or that tan areola surrounding it as well, just keep licking. And do not trail your tongue up and down the butt crack, because that actually tickles most women. Believe me I've learned that from experience. After you've provided this oral contact with her sexy anus, she may place her hand under her and start masturbating, which is a direct sign she is wishing you would go further and deeper between her buttocks. And she might even reach back and pull her cheeks open wide for you to have better access. This is another non spoken plea for more direct contact with her butthole.

At this point, after she's made done everything except beg you to lick her ass, trace a line with your tongue around her brown areola ... then start painting this tender flesh of her areola. At this point, if she doesn't utter a sound, and doesn't move ...then just back off. But if she does utter a soft moan ... that is an invitation to sample that sweet hole of hers.

Lightly at first, run your tongue across that tender opening, down to her perineum. This is also a very sensitive area in most men and women. She may start moaning at this time, lightly, constantly, simply because you have taken the time to build a fire in her body ... not to mention yours as well. Gently caress her perineum, slowly getting stronger with your tongue. Probably at this point, her masturbation will get stronger, releasing her hold on her buttocks. So ... that you will have to separate her cheeks yourself to give her asshole the further attention it is needing.

At this point, you may start licking her butthole, or rolling your tongue around and over this nether opening until her butthole is very wet from your saliva. Then ... when she is least expecting it you may start licking this opening heavily, using broad strokes with your tongue. She may from time to time clench her buttocks together, and then push her butt back into your face. She is all yours at this point so go for the gusto and go back to licking her sweet tight hole again.

But, if you are more interested in tasting deeper pleasures, you might go ahead and thrust your tongue deeply up the rear orifice. If you really start to get into it, just keep licking until she reaches an explosive orgasm and once again relaxes on the bed.

This whole procedure that you do should have taken at least one solid hour from start to finish. If you're like me, I absolutely adore receiving pleasure from my anus. Whether it is anal licking or finger fucking I love getting it in the ass. I would do it every day if possible ...but sadly my hemorrhoids from having children won't let me.

Also, I must say that it should not be done with the receiving partner lying on her tummy throughout the entire time. Variety is the true spice of life, so have her assume several different positions for this.

For instance, when she is lying on her tummy, simply have her roll unto her side and have her pull one leg up high towards her breasts, her upper leg. Her lower leg should remain straight. This position opens her butt up wider for you, and you can see the 'heart shape' of her rump. Or she may wish to take the upper position, or the more dominant position. In this position, she may masturbate more freely as you're under her adoring her butthole. My husband once licked my asshole for at least one and half hours while in vacation in this position. We took a shower together and he cleaned my ass really good and as I laid on the bed and lifted my leg he went to work with his tongue.

During the hour you have been doing this, she will have received no less than three strong orgasms. It is an act that leaves no boundaries ... no limit on the total ecstasy you might perform.

So ... enjoy yourself. Find out exactly what I'm talking about ... if you dare!

Chapter 10

Moving From Analingus To Anal Fingering

What About Analingus

As we have said before engaging in analingus or any anal play for that matter, make sure to thoroughly wash the anal area really good. Once it's clean, licking this area of the body is virtually no different than licking any other part of their body. Also, it can be very stimulating for your partner. Like other types of sexual play in this area, don't just jump right in, but build up the excitement for them and allow your partner to get really comfortable. As we have said a great way to start performing analingus is to move into it when you are performing fellatio or cunnilingus. In fact, that was the first time my rosebud was ever touched with a tongue when my husband was going down on me and he moved down and starting rimming around my asshole with his tongue. The move felt so great, and I found myself pushing my ass back into his face. It caught me off guard at first and I jumped. But as he kept probing the area that was really sensitive, so as he ran his tongue around in circular motions, using his tongue to tickle me, and when I was ready for it, he began to penetrate me.

It is true that the anus is a little tougher than his penis, but there are several positions that are ideal for analingus and fingering. These three seem to be the best. Having them lying on their back with a large pillow to arch their bum up. Or have them bend over with their legs spread. Or have them standing up with you on your knees behind them spreading their cheeks with your hands.

I know this book is about giving your lover pleasure with your tongue. But you must also learn to move on from licking the anus, to finding other ways to pleasure your mate. As we have already said there are two very pleasurable spots in and around the human anus. The first location is the anus itself; it is surrounded by a large number of nerve bundles and is very sensitive. The second in the male is the prostate gland; it is located a few inches inside the anus towards the belly button, and often feels like a firm bulge.

Let's Talk About Getting Started

I have to tell you right off the bat that some men are not very open to experimentation with this body part and enjoying it may make them question their sexuality. As stupid as this all may sound, it is a result of prejudice thinking and lack of understanding in today's society. In any event, make sure to take the time to communicate with your partner to avoid any bad reactions they may have. If your partner refuses, don't force him, but try to open them up to the idea by exploring the area more often with your hands and tongue. If it's a man he'll slowly get used to being touched around there, and it won't seem like such a big deal to them. And remember, by stimulating his prostate gland properly as he gets close to cumming, you can give him an orgasm three or even more times as intense!

As we have said, cleanliness is also essential with virtually all kinds of this form of play. So, taking an erotic bath or a shower is a great primer to this type of play. This type of play can also be the start of sexual festivities. Once your finger(s) or a sex toy has been inside his anus, don't put them anywhere else until you wash them. Carelessness in this regard can cause a very serious infection. So, make sure to have a good lubricant, and start as slowly as possible the first few times.

Also be sure to clip your fingernails quite short before doing any type of penetration, especially anal penetration. The lining of the rectum is really thin and can be torn by sharp objects. So, sister if you have longer fingernails, you can pack some cotton balls around your fingernails and put on a finger cot or latex glove.

Let's Get To Fingering

Once you get them completely lubricated, you want to start by taking it really easy at first. Most people who have never had any anal play will tense their sphincter muscles up at any sign of intrusion. If they are tensing, do not try to push through, as it will cause a lot of pain and discomfort.

Instead, make little circles around their anus and wait for them to relax. Once they starts relaxing, gently try moving your finger in and out a little. Start shallow and slowly move deeper, just make sure to watch his reactions and facial expressions to see if you are going too fast.

Once you get inside, you can do a variety of things, including twisting your hand a little, pulling in and out, moving in large circles following the wall of the anal cavity, or stimulating specific spots with little circles. The most effective use of anal play is definitely right at the point of their orgasm. If you have a lubed finger inside stimulating his prostate when he reaches an orgasm, you will send him to another world of pleasure. One that he will most likely be asking you to help him revisit. He will also shoot more cum with the stimulation of his prostate at that point since most of the cum in manufactured in the prostate gland. For her she will absolutely go wild and crazy if you stimulate her clit as you finger pump her anus.

What About Anal Intercourse

Anal sex is quite a different ball game when you are using something other than your finger. Even if they enjoy anal play and request you to pleasure them there, they may be apprehensive about putting something so large as a dildo or hard cock in there. The keys to success are sufficient in this area and are quite simple. Go Slow, I mean really slow and use copious amounts of lubrication. Relaxation on their part, and yes, a slow, gentle approach. Let him tell you when they want it harder or faster and don't be shy about playing with his penis or her clit at the same time.

Using Anal Toys

What About Butt Plugs

A butt plug is a toy that is slowly inserted in the rectum. Once it is inserted, you can leave it where it is or move it in and out. Many people enjoy the sense of fullness that butt plugs bring, much in the same way women enjoy the fullness experienced during vaginal sex. Others enjoy the sensation of inserting something in their anus.

Butt plugs come in many different shapes and sizes. Some of the sizes seem silly, but some people are obsessed with larger toys, so the companies willingly accommodate. The most popular plugs are less than an inch in diameter, and roughly around 4 inches long.

Climax Beads

These beads are some of the most popular anal toys. They range from soft to firm-textured, and usually consist of four to ten balls connected with a piece of nylon cord or plastic/rubber, and there are a wide selection of ball sizes. Whichever type you are interested in, these are virtually the best toys to ease into anal play with.

Climax beads are a very simple toy to use. After being covered by a good lubricant, they are inserted into the anus slowly bead by bead. Most people then leave the beads where they are until near the point of orgasm, at which time the beads are slowly pulled out one by one. This can greatly intensify an orgasm to the point that it is too intense to handle. I suggest starting with smaller balls, and then carefully moving up, as you get more experienced.

And like everything else involved with anal play, cleanliness is of the highest importance. Make sure to clean your toy thoroughly after using it, store it in a dry dust free place, and be very gentle when starting out.

Other Anal Sex Moves

If your lover seems a little shy when it comes to new things in the bedroom, a great way to bring up the idea of sex toys is to casually bring up the issue in a non-sexual environment. This way, it's really conversational and non-threatening. It is easy to find articles in all types of magazines that discuss the use of sex toys between couples and may help them to see that this is not a unusual act, but a well-accepted one that in no way threatens his masculinity, or her femininity, nor criticizes any of your past experiences together. Sex toys are now widely excepted and readily available; the world is starting to realize that sex toys offer a unique way to explore our body as well as our partners and can add a great twist to a regular sex routine.

Another very erotic and tantalizing way to get them involved is to let them watch you use your toys. Many men love to watch women masturbate, especially when he knows he can join in. So, touch yourself in front of him and bring out your favorite toy. Maybe even let him use your toy on you; tell him where you like it put and what you like, or what you want, and how it makes you feel. Then, if he seems open to the idea, ask him if you can give him a turn. If he says yes, great, if not, don't give up sometimes these things take a little while to get used to. Now it's finally time to enter the world of boys' toys.

The sometimes-taboo area of male stimulation is the prostate gland. Your guy may or may not be into this. If he's not sure, sometimes slow progress is a great way to go. Start by just doing a lot of ass play. Then the next time you two are together try some anus stimulation without any probing. After that he may be interested in a small amount of finger insertion. Just take things slow and he'll soon let you know whether it is an area of pleasure or not.

Here we'll look at a comfortable technique for giving him extra stimulation if he's interested. From either in front or behind of him, stimulate his anus to help the muscles relax. Just as with anal sex it is important that the anus be relaxed, and only gentle pressure be used to avoid both physical and psychological injury. Make sure you apply plenty of lube before very slowly and gently inserting your index finger up to the second knuckle. Curve your finger slightly towards his penis from inside. This should allow you to touch his prostate. For continued stimulation use a "come here" type motion against his prostate, tap it lightly, or slide your finger or a toy in and out of the rectum, achieving the same type of stimulation. For your own protection or comfort finger cots or disposable gloves can also be used, again with lots of lubrication. Be careful not to use a lubricant that may break down the materials of the glove or the finger cot.

If these tricks do the job to get him interested in sex toys, or if you would like to start with something a little more adventurous.   There are endless possibilities from these toys girls! Let's find out how we can use these toys on our boys…

Chapter 11

Let's Finish The Book With Another Erotic Scene

Eating Her Sweet Ass

I must admit that I absolutely adore my wife's ass, and she knows it. Best of all, she revels in it with me. She's never afraid to show it to me, offer it to me, and let me lose myself in its warmth and softness while I seek the deeply erotic scents and delicious tastes that lie between her very ample soft butt cheeks. She knows, understands, and thrills at the power that her anus holds over me. It, in turn, is a comfort zone of intense pleasure for her as well.

She's a heavyset woman, about 5-foot-4 and 180 pounds with curly, short hair. Her ass is big and round, yet firm and beautiful. It's the perfect payoff to her wide hips and lush, sexy full figure. The curve of her belly is also quite alluring. Her pussy is almost clean shaven, and her mons is plump and so inviting. The juices between the delicate pink lips of her pussy are buttery and sweet, and I love the time I spend between her big, warm thighs.

But the times we love most are when my face is buried in her warm, nude ass and she is sharing her most intimate, forbidden place with me. She knows she can make my cock ache with anticipation when she teases me with her sexy ass. She sometimes dances slowly and seductively while wearing her black thong nightie with her large sexy breasts hanging out bare for my viewing pleasure. Sometimes she even wears nipple feathers for my viewing pleasure. Then she bends over spreads her cheeks to reveal her sexy anus to me. The big, puckered slit is surrounded by soft, delicately wrinkled dark skin that holds her flavors. She is so deeply excited by the sensation of my tongue on and inside her tender asshole. We have an understanding and comfort level after years of being together that allows me to taste her at any times. She knows my lust is intense when her anus is slick with her pussy juice and slightly moist. The musky iron taste and scent is incredibly arousing after a long day.

The tight ring of her anus relaxes slightly as I lick and suck on it, and she admits me, surrendering to the kinky thrill of my tasting her there. Knowing that I get off on it makes her incredibly horny.

Her asshole is so sensitive to my tongue's play and probing, and her orgasms are strong even when her cunt is not touched. So, she has come to love showing off her ass to me and being rimmed. I more than love pleasuring her in this way. I give her long, slow, sensuous rim jobs at bedtime, or during a back rub, or when I'm giving her a massage on our heated massage table. Or when she is simply just sitting on the couch and watching TV or reading. She often asks for them, and that makes my cock harden by simply appearing before me nude from the waist down. She will immediately turn a simple playfully slap on her big broad ass into an analingus session. She lies on her side with her legs curled, or on her stomach, and I lovingly shower her buttocks with kisses before my tongue finds its way to her savory pucker.

Tonight, she lay curled on her side, wearing only black nylon stockings and eating chocolate wafer sticks. She ran a hand through my hair as I eagerly and lovingly licked her soft, moist cunt working my way down to her asshole. The scent in the cleft of her buttocks was almost intoxicating and her anus was electrifyingly sweet. It made me ravenous, and as the taste soon faded with each swirl of my tongue, I sought for more within her.

The satiny warmth of her sexy plush nude buttocks covered my face completely as I probed and tasted her ass. Her anus relaxed and my tongue was greeted by the pillowy softness within its folds. She purred with pleasure, so I stiffened my tongue and moved it slowly in and out, in and out, like a tiny wet cock. Every so often, I stopped to admire her lovely wet hole, as it relaxed and slightly opened, waiting for more action from my tongue.

When she was finally about to cum, I reached up and took a wafer stick from her. It was somewhat thicker than a pencil and I rubbed it slowly against her anus. The chocolate melting and smearing on her web of delicate wrinkles. I pressed it in gently, as I inserted the candy halfway into her asshole.

"Mmmmmm," she sighed in pleasure of being penetrated by the sugary treat, pulling one of her cheeks up so she could better see in the mirror next to the bed. The chocolate was now sticking out of her anus, and I began to lick at it. Slowly nibbling at the end of the wafer stick, I chewed my way down until only half of it remained inside her ass.

While she was feeling my tongue swirl on her anus, she flexed her pucker a little and pushed the rest of the candy out of her ass and into my hungry waiting mouth. The chocolate was bittersweet, and I savored it, licking the remainder off her tender slit.

As I feasted away at her tender pucker, I felt her opening my belt with her fingers to removed my erect penis, which was soon surrounded by the warmth of her mouth. She sucked intently as I feverishly tongue-fucked her asshole. Within a minute or two, we both came intensely. Her delicate asshole was frantically spasming and clenching my tongue as my warm, sticky cream filled her mouth. It was the perfect dessert for each of us, and we shared a long passionate kiss, exchanging our flavors, fully alive in our sweet intimacy.

If you enjoyed this book why not consider leaving a review where you purchased it. Much Thanks!

Tori Silks

Other Books By Tori Silks

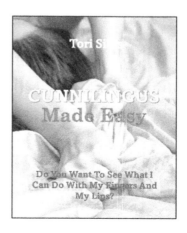

Cunnilingus Made Easy

Does the whole act of giving your wife such great oral sex that it leads to her having a mind-blowing orgasm intimidate you?

Well take it from a lady who knows cunnilingus is perhaps the most enjoyed form of partner sex a women can engage in. For some women it also is the only way that she will be able to have an orgasm. Nothing can compare to the feeling of a warm wet tongue sliding across a woman's soft vulva and clitoris. With the exception of personal masturbation, cunnilingus oral sex probably results in more female orgasms than any other sexual practice.

And contrary to common belief, and in tune with the woman's many expectations, cunnilingus is not a natural skill that every man is born with. Cunnilingus is by far a learned skill. I can say this for a fact, because my husband has gotten so much better of the years of our marriage. If you do not take the time to learn this skill, your wife will never fully enjoy the benefits of it. Every woman is different, so no matter how good someone was at giving a woman oral pleasure in the past, they may still need to relearn their technique if they change partners. There are physical and psychological reasons for this of course. While everyone would like to read a detailed "How-To-Guide," there is no way of creating one that is accurate for all women. At most, one can only give you specific techniques and basic hints in finding your way through your women's wonderland.

And that's what this book "Cunnilingus Made Easy" is all about. Finding and reading your women's reactions to your new ideas and techniques is perhaps the best way to see what she likes. But the individual woman is the only person who can tell you what is enjoyable for her and what works best for her.

You will learn not how to not only use your mouth and tongue, but also how to use your fingers and thumb to bring her extreme oral pleasure. There are certain things that if you do them right, you will have her climbing the walls and bucking in your face and even squirting across the room if you know what to do. **So, give your wife a great orgasm tonight and get a copy of Cunnilingus Made Easy. Buy a copy today!**

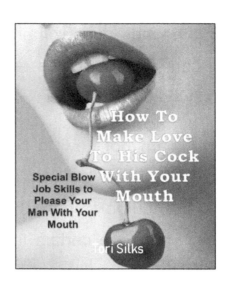

How To Worship Your Man's Cock With Your Mouth

So, you want to learn how to suck dick properly?

You came to the right place and bought the right book!

So, listen up. In this book, I'll give you some simple, step by step tips that will immediately make you better at sucking dick than at least three fourths of other chicks out there that have NO IDEA how to suck a cock properly. Your guy will faint from pleasure because you are not just sucking his cock, but you are making love to it and actually worshipping his cock with your mouth.

Knowing that If you have a perfect technique for sucking dick – all of that will be worth NOTHING if your attitude STINKS. You have to MASTER the winning attitude that turns your man on to give the proper blow job that all men want. So just what is that attitude that is needed?

No – it's NOT just being enthusiastic about having a dick in your mouth. It's much more than that. You have to show him that you ADORE his dick more than life itself.

Look at his dick with pure lust and fascination in your eyes, as if you went NUTS and you are having MULTIPLE-SQUIRTING-ORGASMS from simply having your lips wrapped around his dick. Sucking dick should be an art, a passion, a love-at-first sight dick kind of adventure.

If you don't have what it takes to acquire a perfect cock-sucker's attitude, then it's better if you don't suck on his cock at all. Jerking off will be more pleasurable for him. But if you do want to blow his mind by blowing his cock then this book is for you. This book will teach you how to develop a relationship with his cock. A relationship that is like worship.

Look – ANY chick can learn how to suck dick properly, it's easy. Just master a couple of good techniques, learn the right pace you should suck at, apply the right amount of pressure and that's it. It's not a rocket-science. But blowjobs like that will always be just MEDIOCRE. They'll never be a memorable experience to him. They'll never be something that he'll remember as a 90-year-old man with Alzheimer disease.

And when it comes to sucking his dick like a true professional – that's what you should aim for. You should offer your man world class cock sucking because he deserves your best. Trust me lady your man will ADORE you for it. Really – I'm serious there's nothing more powerful for a man than a great blow job.

The benefits of knowing how to suck dick amazingly are beyond measure. You'll have a deeper more intimate relationship with him than ever before.

But when it comes to powerful orgasms, where he's hitting the wall and his eyes are POPPING out from pleasure – You MUST please him on a PSYCHOLOGICAL level first.

That's what cock worship does. That's MUCH more important and harder to master.

If you can do that – every blow job, you give him will be MIND-BLOWING. That's why it's called mind-blowing – because his MIND blows up! His brain cells EXPLODE from pleasure.

THAT is where man's truly powerful orgasms happen. In his head. Not just in his dick. That's what so many of you girls totally forget about. You have to seduce his big head first, then you can work on the little head.

Learn how to suck dick in a way so that you please his MIND and conquer it – get SO deep into his memory that he'll never forget your blow job. That should be your goal. I'll teach you how to do that. Get Your copy of **How To Make Love To His Cock With Your Mouth Today!** Buy it Now!

Made in the USA
Las Vegas, NV
04 October 2024

96277305R00046